This book belongs to

DOUBLEDAY

New York   London   Toronto
Sydney   Auckland

Amy

the
Dancing
Bear

Carly Simon

Illustrated by Margot Datz

PUBLISHED BY DOUBLEDAY
a division of Bantam Doubleday Dell Publishing Group, Inc.
666 Fifth Avenue, New York, New York 10103

DOUBLEDAY and the portrayal of an anchor with a dolphin
are trademarks of Doubleday, a division of
Bantam Doubleday Dell Publishing Group, Inc.

CIP Data applied for

ISBN 0-385-26637-5
ISBN 0-385-26721-5 (lib. bdg.)

FIRST EDITION

BOOK MARK

The text of this book was set in
the typeface Bernhard Modern
by Maxwell Typographers, New York, New York.

The color was separated by
Action Nicholson Color, Brook Park, Ohio.

It was printed on 80 lb Michigan Matte
by WA Krueger Company New Berlin Book Division,
New Berlin, Wisconsin.

Designed by Marysarah Quinn

To my mother, Andrea
and my daughter, Sally

—C.S.

To my mother, Joan
and my daughter, Scarlet

—M.D.

It was almost Amy's bedtime and she probably knew it. Her mother, a large and graceful bear, appeared in Amy's doorway and said, "Amy, my darling girl, though the moon is not yet so high in the sky, it is time you changed into your nightgown or nightshirt or whatever you're wearing to bed these days."

"Mother," pleaded Amy, "the sun is still coming through the trees. It is filtered and dappled and the air still smells of fresh-mown hay. Please let me dance here in my room until the moon is a little higher and the sun a little lower. I'm so happy with my pirouettes and so filled with joy!"

*H*ow could her mother argue with that? How could she cut short this delight, this artful little creature with her sunny auburn curls and her graceful turns like tropical palms moving in the wind? So she spoke in a practical tone: "Amy, I will go

into the kitchen and I'll wash all the dishes. When I come back in here, I would like
to see you ready for bed."

"Thank you, Mother." Amy threw her hands off in another direction and the
rest of her body followed.

my's mother went into the kitchen and washed each glass, plate, and even polished the knives and forks with a special pink polish until each was so shiny you could see your reflection in it if you felt like it. Then she returned to Amy's room.

"Amy." Her mother's voice was more stern. "I don't see that anything has changed."

"Dear Mother, the sun has turned to gold and my room is filled with the magic of twilight. There is nothing I couldn't invent in here now. No step too difficult for my body to take. The birds are only beginning their goodnight songs and this is just the music I have waited for. I am so inspired and not in the least bit tired. Please, oh please, let me just dance a little more, just a little more."

Her mother, who was charmed by her daughter, could again hardly refuse such a pleasant little argument, so she spoke with motherly understanding: "Darling girl, you are nearly incorrigible but this is the last time. I shall go into the living room and listen to one side of a piano sonata and then when I return, I shall expect to find you in bed. I mean between the sheets!"

And with that command, she went into the living room and found her favorite record and put it on the turntable and sat back in the sofa with a cool glass of iced

tea. *As certain as the piano sonata was over in seventeen minutes, so Amy's mother was certain she would find her daughter at least in her nightgown, nightshirt, or pajamas. But sometimes Amy's mother was wrong.*

When she came a third time into Amy's room, Amy was in the middle of a tango with an imaginary partner, her eyes glowing and turned toward the evening sky. "Amy, you know I am not harsh or strict and never utter a sound that resembles a bark in your direction, but really my child, you push me to the limit. Next you'll be asking me if you can stay up dancing until the sun rises in the East!"

"I know you think I am disobedient and disrespectful, but sometimes, Mother, my spirit rises and something in me says, 'Stay right where you are!'

"Do you see the moon and how it appears at the horizon? Look at the lightning bugs and then the same twinkling farther up in the sky of the early stars. I feel I can

float through arabesques, and when the night mists drift through the window on the soft night breeze it makes me want to dance forever. Can you believe how happy I must be?"

*W*ell, if only everybody could feel that way. Since it was summer and there was no school, Amy's mother decided not to scold Amy. Instead, her voice was low and gentle: "All right, my darling dancing little bear, dance on. I'll be in the bathtub. I'll come in when I'm washed and dry and by then you'll be quite tired." Amy was so happy that her mother understood that she gave a low curtsy and then jumped impishly into her mother's arms for a big hug.

my's mother, always somewhat of a sport, moved sleepily into the bathroom, where she ran a bath, adding foam of apple blossoms so that the bubbles finally rose higher than the edge of the tub itself. When she got into this fine warm bath, she lay her head back and let herself relax very deeply. She began to think of Uncle Harry and his

watch that never told the time. She thought about her recipe for baked Alaska and she thought about piano sonatas. She thought about Amy and how much she really loved to dance. As she was thinking about the red woolen mittens she planned to knit for next fall, she drifted off into the kind of peaceful sleep that only happy thoughts can give rise to.

ama, dearest Mother—
dear, oh dear, it must be so late,
you've fallen to sleep in the tub!"
Amy smiled down at her mother as if
she were her own precious little baby.
"Come on, it's time to go to bed, let
me help you dry off." Amy reached,
still in her dance, for a big soft towel
that was hanging on a hook nearby.
Coming out of her dreams for a
minute, Amy's mother parted the
bubbles as she stepped out of the tub.

After she was all dry and snuggled into a loose-fitting blue nightie, Amy's mother, still blinking back sleep, let Amy lead her into her big cozy bed. Amy tucked the covers around her mother and opened the window just wide enough to let a stream of cool honeysuckled air into the room.

As she kissed her mother goodnight,
her mother kissed her back and
noticed that Amy was finally dressed
in her pajamas. She noticed, too,
that the moon was high in the sky
and that the stars gathered into a
constellation, designed by the heavens,

to form one perfectly happy,
perfectly tireless,
perfectly wonderful
dancing bear.